I0676738

Hope in a Bottle

By
Neil O'Donnell

Argus Enterprises International Inc
New Jersey***North Carolina

Hope in a Bottle © 2012

All rights reserved by Neil O'Donnell.

No part of this book may be reproduced or transmitted in any form or by any means, graphic, electronic, or mechanical, including photocopying, recording, taping, or by any informational storage retrieval system without prior permission in writing from the publisher.

A-Argus Better Book Publishers, LLC
For information:
A-Argus Better Book Publishers, LLC
9001 Ridge Hill Street
Kernersville, North Carolina 27285
www.a-argusbooks.com

ISBN: 978-0-6155849-4-2
ISBN: 0-6155849-4-2

Book Cover designed by Dubya
Printed in the United States of America

Dedication

To Konstantinos "Gus" Koutsandreas, whose support and guidance helped so many of us get our start in life. You will never be forgotten, Gus.

~ Ned and Neil O'Donnell

There is always Hope...

To the parishioners of St. Bonaventure Parish in West Seneca:

In remembering our parish, and by holding true to our faith and the missions our community held dear, St. Bonaventure Church will live on. God bless you all.

Prologue

It was to be a rewarding day. Yet, Debra found her waiting and the inevitable elation bittersweet; her mother would not be there to share in the moment.

Sitting on her front steps, Debra braved the nippy autumn morning to stand watch, awaiting the arrival of the day's mail. While the chill of the air and the cement steps made her vigil uncomfortable, heat from the sun's rays that periodically pierced the clouds, along with draws from her coffee mug, helped her endure. The wait was not so terrible. The sounds of the fall season in Lancaster, New York, her home since birth, brought about happy memories. The sounds of lawn mowers and leaf blowers aside, Debra enjoyed the sound of children laughing as they dove into piles of leaves recently shed from their respective trees. The scent of burning leaves and wood burning fireplaces added to the nostalgia, providing additional comfort as her wait continued.

"Nothing like a western New York autumn," Debra said, letting the air carry her words to no one in particular, words her mother said throughout Debra's life. For long moments, she again went through memories of her mother. They were like twins, each with long, auburn hair, blue eyes and a slight frame that reached a height of five feet, five inches. Debra smirked, thinking of all the times people mistook her and her mother for sisters. The brief moment of joy was soon replaced by the reality of her mother's death seven months earlier.

The heart attack was unexpected for a 54 year old who otherwise appeared healthy. Debra came home to find her mother on the floor, unresponsive. For three days, her mother remained in a coma before finally passing away in the early hours of the morning.

"I miss you, Mom," Debra said aloud, fighting back the tears now welling up in her eyes. The familiar screech of the mail truck pulled her attention back to her vigil and the joy she awaited. Remaining seated, Debra watched the mail carrier stop at each of the three mailboxes that preceded hers. The squeal of the brakes and the sound of mailboxes opening and closing played in concert with the hum of the mail truck's engine as it powered the oddly designed truck between stops. Finally, the mail truck stopped at Debra's mailbox. Positioned nearly eighty feet from her house, Debra felt the mailbox might as well be a mile away for the time it took for this delivery to arrive. Then, after the mail carrier shoved Debra's mail into the box, closed the box's lid, waved and drove off, Debra started the walk.

After setting her coffee on the step, Debra walked slowly to her mailbox, feelings of euphoria clashing with the melancholy that seemed to appear every time she anticipated exciting news. Once at the mailbox, Debra rested her hand on the lid, delaying its opening as a flurry of worries went through her mind. *What if it hadn't arrived?* *What if they sent the wrong book?* Debra pushed through those thoughts and opened the lid; the package was there, a life-long dream within. Rushing back to the porch, she grabbed her coffee before heading for the backyard where white flags demarcated the invisible fencing that contained Buster, the beagle puppy she adopted weeks earlier. Tail wagging, Buster ran to Debra's side and jumped on to her lap as she sat in one of the red-stained Adirondack chairs on the back deck.

"Here it is, Mom," Debra said as she rested her hand on the cardboard-entomb paperback she spent years writing. Debra waited several moments examining the package before digging her nails into the tape that barred entry. Then, after a tussle with packing peanuts and shrink-wrap, Debra viewed the first finished copy of her novel, *Rising Son*. Born of her interest in Native American societies, which her mother encouraged,

Debra used the historical fiction framework to detail the forced relocation of Native Americans during the nineteenth century. While working on her Anthropology degree at Buffalo State College, she spent a considerable amount of time visiting museums and historical societies where she examined the diaries and journals of Native Americans forced to relocate and those who orchestrated the action.

"Is that it?" a voice asked, startling Debra. Turning towards the back door, Debra saw her Aunt Becca, who exited the house and sat in one of the other chairs on the deck. After composing herself, Debra answered.

"I read a few chapters to Mom that last day. At least she heard some of it." Becca, Debra's only maternal aunt, looked nothing like her mother. Becca stood six feet tall, had short, blond hair and was rather quiet. Yet, for all the differences, the compassion of their family flowed in Becca as well.

"I have no doubt your mother looked over your shoulder as you read and edited every line of the proof. She's read it, and I know she is so proud of you."

"I just wish I could see her hold it," Debra said in reply. Becca's heart ached for both her sister and her niece. Yet, she could think of no words to console either. Pulling Debra into a hug, Becca let long held tears flee her eyes as Debra did the same. Buster, now calmed a bit, sat and watched his human handlers as they wept. Soon, he too displayed sadness, letting a whimper resonate for a long moment. Aunt and niece both laughed as they turned to look at the sullen beagle whose tail suddenly rocked the small canine body.

"I tell you what," Becca said, as she stood and pulled Debra to her feet. "Your uncle won't be home for a couple hours yet. Why don't I throw a few sandwiches in a backpack and we can go eat lunch and read in Como Park, by the creek? Your mother and I used to do that all the time. I figure you could read a chapter or two to your mom. Sound good?" Debra nodded. Arm in arm, niece and aunt went into the house to prepare their impromptu picnic before heading to the park.

***

Ham and cheese sandwiches, washed down with raspberry iced-tea, preempted a run around the park by Becca and a stroll to the creek bed by Debra. Spreading out a blanket, Debra opened her book to the dedication. The tears came quickly.

"To Mom," she said, reading the words she intended to be a part of every dedication. Flipping to the acknowledgments, Debra looked over the list of people who provided her the support to get through the last few months; her aunt, her agent and the editor who spent ample time making sure the final print was polished and something Debra would be proud of. After finding energy in her supports, Debra started to read aloud the first chapter, laughing at the hidden jokes laced throughout the text, jokes only Debra and her mother would get. Minutes later, the chapter finished, Debra closed the book before looking skyward.

"Can you see this, Mom?" she asked, her sorrow in full swing once more. Debra looked to the water, watching the current for direction away from her thoughts. First, she eyed a fish circling just below the surface. Her eyes then darted to a small branch that glided along the current at a slow and steady pace until it wedged between a cluster of rocks where a plastic, 20 oz pop bottle was likewise trapped. For long moments, she watched the bottle bob in and out of the water, the current and rocks isolating the plastic container to the area. Standing, Debra gained a better view of the bottle. While adhesive and bits of its plastic label remained affixed to the bottle, no discernible marks were visible. Its shape and maroon cap reminded her of the Dr. Pepper she drank daily. Yet, the flavor of the contents failed to interest her once she saw the note inside the bottle. Removing her shoes and rolling up her pant legs, Debra wadded into the cold water, maneuvering over the slick shale that lined the creek bed. Her progress slow, it took nearly ten minutes to bridge the thirty plus feet to the bottle. Once there, she pulled the container from its snare; the seal was intact, but the note inside was folded over so she could not read the message. After unscrewing the cap, Debra wiped her hand on her pant leg before shaking the note out onto her palm. Securing the bottle under her arm, she then opened the note and read aloud its fateful message.

"A mother's pride in her child is all knowing and everlasting!" Tears of hope and joy flooded Debra's eyes as she again looked skyward, peering beyond a lone seagull that circled overhead.

"Thank you, Mom," Debra said. "I love you." In time, Debra framed the note and hung it over the roll top desk where she ultimately penned all her future manuscripts, never once doubting her mother was watching on with pride.

Chapter 1

William Sullivan stared out the back window of the taxi, watching his sisters and brother wave goodbye and then vanish as the taxi turned onto Seneca Street. He could never have imagined it would be the last time he would see them.

William was embarking on a journey to South America to help build schoolhouses and shelters for a remote village devastated by two hurricanes, which pummeled the region in a span of three weeks. Thousands were dead or missing and presumed dead; rescue efforts were now replaced by recovery and reconstruction activities.

William carried with him a leather satchel his brother gave him when he graduated from Buffalo State College. William's studies focused on archaeology, so his older brother thought William needed a bag like what Indiana Jones carried in *Raiders of the Lost Ark*. His crate of clothes and books forwarded the previous day, William only carried two pairs of khakis, three pair of socks, three pair of boxers, and two white, long sleeved, button-down trail shirts like those travelers wore on safaris. For comfort and distraction, he tucked a vinyl case amongst his clothes, which contained his two most cherished books along with the rosary he received on his First Communion. With a pair of deck shoes, a journal, and a few pens stuffed into a side compartment, William felt prepared for the journey south, though anxiety over his work consumed him. Would he be able to provide comfort for those who grieved? Would he be able to withstand the death spread throughout the region? Would he bring hope to those he served? Answers to his questions would come soon enough.

After reaching the airport, William headed into line to be scanned and questioned about his travels. After thirty minutes of waiting and removing and redonning his belt and shoes, he walked straight to the terminal after first getting a cup of McDonald's coffee.

"Last chance for the good stuff," William said as he choked the coffee with sugar and milk before taking a seat outside the gate. He leaned far back in his chair and gazed at the disorganized activity that consumed the runway just outside the windows. People, fuel trucks and carted luggage appeared to encroach on each other's space leading to a frenzy of curses the terminal's glass windows failed to silence.

"Great view," William muttered before taking a few sips from his coffee.

"Traveling far, Father?" an elderly woman asked as she sat in the chair across from William. Suddenly very aware of the collar about his neck and his black suit, William was taken aback. His ordination just days earlier, he still found the title an awkward change years in the seminary failed to prepare him for.

"I'll be above the clouds for the better part of the next two days," he said as he considered the trek to a Brazilian village he first heard of only weeks earlier.

"At least you'll be closer to God, Father," she said, before she pulled out a book, ending their impromptu conversation.

"Indeed," William replied as he returned his attention to the chaos outside.

***

Never a fan of flying, William clawed into his armrests as the mounting storm jilted the twin prop plane carrying him on the last leg of his journey. Seven others, the pilot included, struggled to stay in their seats. The plane, appearing to have been last serviced by the Wright brothers, had the aerodynamics of a semi-trailer, which explained why passengers and crew alike gripped onto their seats as if their hands were vices. However, with the plane lacking constraining seatbelts, several passengers were thrown to the cabin floor by the conflict between inertia and gravity. For the first time in his life, William actually saw passengers use the vomit-bags the airline provided.

"Please, please stay in your seats!" the pilot called out over the intercom, first in Spanish and then in English. "We should be out of the storm soon." Based on the pilot's distraught tone, William guessed things were about to get a lot worse. Gripping the armrests tighter, William peered out the window by his seat looking for any sliver of hope the plane would reach calm skies. Yet, the craft seemed to head only deeper into the mix of grey and black clouds. A number of passengers, William included, started praying, seeking hope through their collective faith.

Then suddenly, all hope vanished.

Lightning struck, seemingly at several parts of the plane simultaneously, and for an instant, the world seemed on fire. Another bolt then struck the tail section, shearing off several outer plates and forcing the plane into an upward climb, stalling the engines. At the mercy of the growing winds, the plane somersaulted before plunging into a dive. Amidst the screams of the other passengers, William heard the pilot cursing the plane, and for a second, the young priest watched the pilot pull back on the yoke in a last ditch effort to level the aircraft's descent. Then, all was quiet.

Not a sound resonated through William's ears as his mind latched on his childhood home and the image of yellow, burnt orange and crimson leaves falling from the maples lining the property's borders. He walked between the two silver maples nearest the house where he spent many autumn afternoons reading and writing. The sun gleaming, William felt at peace.

"So this is Heaven," William whispered as he reached to catch one of the leaves mid flight. The leaf gently rested in his hand, its descent ended.

"Padre!" cried out a voice in his mind. "Padre!" called out the voice again, this time pulling William from his vision back to reality.

Tepid salt water slapped William seconds before the lone flight attendant did.

"Get up, Padre! We've gotta go, NOW!" She had already pulled William to his feet. Emergency lights, few and far between, provided the only illumination, but it was enough to see the water rising as quickly as people were exiting the plane. Suddenly the plane rocked, knocking William into the now empty seat across from his. His satchel, jarred loose by the plane's abrupt movements, fell from the overhead storage compartments and into his lap.

"Ahora, Padre!" the flight attendant screamed as she rushed towards the nearest exit. Slinging the bag over his shoulder, William struggled towards the doorway where the pilot now stood, the only other person remaining on the plane. The pilot wasted no time. He grabbed William, pushing the young priest out the doorway before exiting himself; they both fell beneath the turbulent waves bombarding the sinking aircraft.

For long moments, William was lost in the cool, churning ocean, not knowing which direction the water's surface lay. Fate intervened once more as he felt something grab hold of his left arm and pull him above water.

"Father, are you all right?" the pilot asked as William fought for air amidst his coughing up salt water. He nodded after a moment as his breath grew regular in pace.

"We're all here, captain!" the flight attendant exclaimed as the pilot grabbed onto the nearest of two inflatable rafts now bobbing in the water. She smiled at the captain; at least they all survived the crash.

"Where's the third raft?" the pilot asked, only seeing two small rafts overburdened with passengers.

"It had a tear; it sank!" she replied, the smile now gone. The last raft had barely room for one more occupant.

"Father, get in! Leave your bag!" the pilot exclaimed as he started to lift William by his collar. "Tell my wife and daughters, I love them!" he yelled to the flight attendant. She simply nodded as she pulled on William's collar trying to lift the priest the last couple inches into the raft. Yet, William was not willing to reach the safety of the crowded craft.

Brushing aside the flight attendant's hand, William pushed off the raft and into the grip of the water and the pilot.

"FATHER, GET IN!" the exasperated pilot exclaimed as he tried to lift William back into the raft. Then, for a moment, the winds and water seemed but a distant distraction. The two men, priest and pilot, locked eyes as peace filled them both.

"Your daughters need you," William said, his visage reflecting nothing but calm. William then smiled. "Go," William then said before he pushed away from the pilot and the raft. A giant wave quickly covered the priest, and in its wake, no sight of William remained.

"FATHER!" the pilot called out. Yet, William was beyond earshot. After several long seconds of peering into the darkness, the pilot finally got into the raft where he and the passengers would spend the next day while the storm passed. As the waters calmed and the sun rose, their vision reached greater distances, but there was no sign of Father William Sullivan. After they were rescued and brought to shore, the pilot immediately contacted William's family, an action he dreaded but knew he alone must do. The sole casualty of the crash, William's family took some solace from knowing that their brother's final act saved the pilot. The pilot, meanwhile, made his way home to be with his family. He swore he would remember the priest always. Like William's family, the pilot offered remembrances to William throughout the rest of his life, speaking of how the young priest had kept him whole for his family. They collectively toasted William's life, never knowing William's life was far from over.

Chapter 2

The wave drove William away from the rafts and into the heart of the storm, where calm reigned. It was surreal for the young priest. All about him waves churned, casting cream tops across every wave, while stars above cast a luminous veil revealing hope. Wreckage from the plane floated about William including two life vests, a trench coat and a number of bags of chips and peanuts. He attempted to reach for the nearest life vest first, but William struggled to swim; William's satchel, surprisingly still slung over his shoulder, made it difficult to propel himself through the water. After adjusting to the satchel's bulk, William made it to the life vest, which he then pulled over his head before tying its attached straps about his waist.

"Thank God!" William exclaimed as a bit of relief set in. It was short lived as the zone of calm started to collapse. Fearing a loss of the bounty floating about, William swam straight for the food, which he clumsily gathered and stuffed into his satchel's main compartment. Then, after slinging the second life vest over his shoulder, William reached the coat.

"Never turn aside a gift from God," William said as he gathered the beige coat into a ball and pulled it to his chest, just before the calm collapsed; William was back in the storm. The next few hours he rode out an amalgamation of torrid winds, pelting rain and monstrous waves, the latter of which routinely knocked the wind out of William. He vowed to fight on as long as God gave him strength, determination that helped him shake off the storm's fury throughout the night. Yet, fear of reality remained ever-present.

As a child, William thought of pursuing marine biology to study sharks or archaeology to study America's prehistoric past. His interest in archaeology won out in college, but his knowledge of sharks remained extensive given his years reading everything he could about sharks from encyclopedia articles to books. That knowledge told him to worry. Miles from any coast, William knew the nearest "man-eating" shark likely swam only yards away and would notice the priest after the seas calmed. Once the storm passed, the race of the searchers would begin. William's hope was in any rescuers sent by the airlines, but his money was on the sharks.

Hours passed as did the storm. By the time the sun crept over the horizon, the clouds were sparse and the waves placid; perfect conditions for spotting planes or dorsal fins.

"Mother of God," William uttered as the sun first fully broke above the water. With wisps of stratus clouds the only obstructions, the sun cast its orange-yellow rays virtually unchallenged, an awe-inspiring sight William would remember always. Then terror struck.

The water's surface exploded behind William, jarring him from his thoughts and causing him to twist around and hold out the balled up jacket for protection. He extended the jacket just in time to deflect a charging, wayward tuna. William laughed.

"I guess that makes me the *chicken of the sea*," he mused as his breathing slowed within norm. Once calmed, William determined he should keep up his strength. Pulling his satchel above the water's surface, he scanned into the main pocket where he placed the chips and peanuts recovered from the plane crash. The effort uncovered a half-empty bottle of Pepsi. Parched, his favorite drink seemed appealing, but the caffeine posed another threat; dehydration.

"Well, it's got water in it," he said before taking a swig of the cola. The acidic liquid burned its way down William's throat. He then recapped the twenty-four ounce bottle before pulling out and opening a bag of peanuts. "Starve or dehydrate?" he asked himself before ingesting a mouthful. He spit out the peanuts seconds later as a dorsal fin broke the surface of the water heading straight for him. William froze. The fin swam closer. Thirty feet... Twenty feet... Ten feet...

The fin's owner, a seven foot, blue shark, vaulted out of the water, propelled by the upward rush of a bottle-nosed dolphin. After splashing back into the sea, the shark moved off.

"You, you don't see that everyday," William said between breaths. Then, just when his breathing settled, a new visitor stole it.

A dolphin's snout popped out of the water five feet from him, chattering on like a long-lost, old friend. Soon three other dolphins joined in the conversation while another two jumped out of the water, their course set towards the fleeing shark.

"I don't suppose any of you speak English?" William asked. The dolphins just continued chatting, their message still indecipherable. William, for a moment, laughed at his company before his heart broke and tears flowed from his eyes, which silenced the dolphins. After bobbing in the water for a few more seconds, the dolphins disappeared into the blue.

"Don't go! PLEASE!" William attempted to swim on in their direction, but his bulk and lack of fins made pursuit impossible. "WAIT!" William cried out, as frustration and hopelessness took hold again. Yet, the awe of the moment returned within seconds as one of the dolphins broke the water's surface and appeared to fly. "A life's worth of wonder in minutes," William thought. He laughed and then looked skyward. "Thank you."

As if in response, a dolphin rose out of the water at William's side and began nudging into the priest with his pectoral fin. Befuddled, William reached out slowly to pet the dolphin's head, but the dolphin did not cease prodding him in the gut with its fin. Curious, William gently, but firmly, grasped the dolphin's dorsal fin after which the dolphin propelled itself forward. Twice William lost his grip, and both times the dolphin returned for him. In time, the dolphin slowed before diving away from William; another dolphin then appeared to takes its place. The rotation of members of the pod continued for what seemed like hours until an island appeared on the horizon.

Chapter 3

William's flight with the dolphins brought unique awareness to the priest. Previously concerned with potential predators lurking in the depths and signaling rescue craft, William never truly observed the ocean itself. His journey with the dolphin pod changed that.

The water was a rich, deep hue of blue unlike anything he ever observed, almost a melding of a summer sky and the feathers of the blue birds that often visited his backyard in Buffalo. Looking down, the edge of his vision registered a darkness beyond midnight, with only a hint of any shade of blue remaining. He suddenly feared that depth. What lay beyond in the darkness?

Light soon broke through the depths, casting shadows over the canyon walls now visible to his tired, brown eyes. Dividing his gaze between the depths and the approaching island, William watched as the distant ocean floor gave way to sand dunes punctuated by schools of unknown species, merely specks to his eyes. The submerged terrain then jumped up towards William and his companions; they were now less than fifty yards from the beach. Abruptly, the dolphin he rode bolted away, leaving William to tread in water just over seven feet deep. Looking around, he watched as the curved dorsal fins of the dolphins danced amidst the waves, almost as if they were playing chase.

"Thank you," William said, before turning towards the beach and swimming the remaining distance. With the trench coat wrapped around his left hand and the extra life vest straddling his right shoulder, the effort was awkward, but progressing. William heard chirping sounds vocalized by the pod, which seemed to move in pace with the priest.

"Let's see you swim with this stuff," William said between breaths, wondering if the chirps were bursts of laughter from his companions.

He reached the shallows minutes after he started his crawl. The moment his shoes touched the pliable sand, William relaxed his arms before sprinting to the beach where he collapsed.

"Thank you, Father," William whispered as he kissed the dry land before flipping over onto his back. Up towards the sky he looked, squinting as the sunlight reached out to everything. "Thank you, God," he said once more as his breathing calmed. Above, seagulls soared, calling out as if in welcome. He knew he was safe.

Chirping from the ocean dragged William from his meditations. Propping himself up, the now sand-covered priest from the Buffalo Diocese looked out towards his rescuers who were jumping out of the water twenty yards from shore. He stood up and ran to the water's edge, his arms waving in jubilation.

"THANK YOU!" William cried as he watched the pod move off to the north. "Bless you my friends," he then whispered before a sudden sadness overwhelmed him. William was now alone.

***

A chill wind raked across the island finding every crevice amidst the foliage and rock that called the land home. At its peak, the wind generated a hollow whistle as it crossed the leaves and grasses. Scanning the landscape, William struggled to identify the vegetation. Certainly not the mixed forests of western New York, yet a familiar peace filled the air. Then, as if on cue from the conductor, birds added their whistles to the unfolding symphony. The lonely island now seemed rich with life, and William instantly felt at home.

"Well, time to explore," William said as he started to remove the clothes he had worn for days. Every bit of clothing he had was wet, but putting on a different shirt and pair of pants was refreshingly affirming life as the dead don't change clothes. First rinsing clean of the sand he accumulated in the surf, William put on one of his travel shirts, a pair of khakis and his deck shoes. Then, while stuffing his black, priest garments into the satchel, William came across a baseball cap he forgot he packed. The worn cap was his father's and bore a patch from the bakery his father worked for during William's childhood; Arnold's Bakery.

"I miss you, Dad," he said as memories of going on delivery runs with his father remained joyful recollections; stocking supermarket shelves, going to Poor Bob's Restaurant for giant hamburgers, and listening to his father's tales about time spent riding horses and exploring the outdoors of Glenwood. Donning the hat backwards, William flipped through his memories while deciding what to eat for his first substantial "meal" on the island. "I'll have peanuts with a side of potato chips," he joked as he pulled out two snack bags and his bottle of Pepsi, which still contained a few gulps of the drink. Taking his hat off, Father William said grace before devouring the foodstuffs. William then packed up his belongings before heading to the island's interior in search of fresh water and, hopefully, help.

The trek was not easy. The vegetation appeared determined to obstruct any passage along the ground, almost as if to protect some ancient treasure or civilization from would-be invaders. With only his hands as implements, William pulled at vines, bushes and gigantic networks of tree limbs in search of holes he could maneuver through. In what seemed an hour, William covered only about a hundred feet of the mixed forest, a revelation that allowed frustration to set in. In a moment of furry, William ripped into the nearest cluster of vines and pushed forward, which ultimately resulted in him stumbling through the vines and landing soundly on his back.

"Ahhh! There's got to be a better way," William said as he stared upwards towards the poplar and conifer treetops that now appeared like skyscrapers over a city street. The illusion was enhanced by the sudden cry of a seagull that sounded like a taxi driver leaning on his car horn. The gray-winged gull, capped with snow-white feathers, floated down to a branch several feet above the priest before continuing to squawk and call out what William assumed were fits of laughter.

"You've got it easy; all you have to do is flap those wings!" William cursed mildly as he propped himself to rest on his elbows. The seagull took exception with the priest's scolding and flew down to William's chest to register its displeasure. First squawking loudly, the seagull then pecked at William's chest grabbing potato chip crumbs before flying back to its previous perch.

"That's it, keep eating. You'll make a great supper some day," William said, amused at his new companion's lack of table manners. The bird ignored him.

After spending minutes watching the seagull struggle to swallow the crumbs it snagged, William stood up and brushed off sand he accumulated during his fall. "Well, it could be worse," William whispered as he finished brushing his clothes off. The sudden rustling of grass and ferns only feet away told William he was about to find out just how much worse things could get. Backing up a few feet away from the disturbance, William looked for a defensive tool, finally locking his eyes on a fallen branch from a nearby poplar. Picking up the yard-long timber, William gripped it like a baseball bat while praying he had the courage to confront the unseen interloper.

"I think we've got company," William said as he looked up to the seagull. His avian tormentor shook its head as if in response before flying off. "Chicken," William cursed as he tightened his grip on the impromptu club, his knuckles whitened by the sudden loss of blood circulation through his hands. "Better not be a polar bear," William whispered as the mass of foliage before him started to part. The beast from the shadows then revealed its head, teeth exposed.

"AH!" William exclaimed, his whole body quivering. The tiny, gray rabbit that emerged from the grass, meanwhile, seemed indifferent to the human presence as it continued munching on the surrounding blades of grass.

Between heavy gasps for breath, William laughed.

Chapter 4

"Rabbits, and seagulls and sharks, oh my," William joked as he continued onward into the heart of the island's forest. From the time he first set foot on the island, clouds obscured the realm above the treetops, appearing like a mist concealing a villain's castle.

"If there's water, it's there," William reasoned before ever beginning his journey, the priest's destination where the clouds appeared most dense. Then, as the trees grew sparse, the cloud cover lost its hold allowing the priest a better view of the island's interior. The trees gave way to a pond fed by the stream from a mountain. For long moments, William stared at the monstrous landform, which rose several hundred feet into the sky. How could he not see this from the beach?

"Mother of God, pray for us," Father William said before making the sign of the Cross. His mouth agape, Father William stood in silence while taking in the sight. The mountain was a mass of granite and shale, covered with a mix of conifers, most of which the priest could not identify. All about the sky, gulls sailed the ocean air needing little propulsion from their wings. As his gaze lowered, Father William took stock of the resources at the mountain's base. An oblong pond, nearly a hundred feet across and bordered by cornstalks around the eastern edge, covered the bulk of the area.

"Water," William uttered, more in prayer than in observation. Puddles he encountered thus far held only salt water, the taste of which now gnawed at William's stomach. With his Pepsi reserve down to a few sips, William knew this was his last hope, a hope kindled by the presence of corn. His dire need for water clear, William ran to the pond's edge and dropped to his knees. The water, clear and still, gleamed in the growing sunlight. He felt unworthy to disturb the water, but knew he must. Dipping his right hand below the pond's surface, William felt a cool shock crawl up his arm. Yet, after accumulating a series of cuts throughout his ordeal, William sensed no irritation to the healing wounds; hope soared.

"Thank you, Father," William said before lifting a handful of the fresh water to his lips. The taste of the crystal-clear water resonated throughout his body. Seconds later, William dunked his head into the pond to drink his fill.

***

A survey of the pond area provided William some solace. In addition to a unique variety of corn growing adjacent to the eastern shore, the pond contained small fish and a bounty of seaweed; he would not starve. With renewed hope, William sat by the pond and opened a package of peanuts while looking over the mountain. His would-be feast and rest were interrupted seconds after ripping open the peanut bag, the flapping of wings drawing William's attention sky-wards. The seagull had returned.

Landing on a tree branch, the seagull squawked as its webbed feet struggled to grab hold.

"Don't you have somewhere else you can perch?" William asked, still recovering from his last encounter with the contemptuous bird. The seagull said nothing. "You win," William said as he tossed a peanut to his companion. In reaching out for the nut, the bird stumbled, falling down to the dirt before it could control its descent. The seagull soon regained its footing and composure. Shaking off its tumble, the avian acrobat located and consumed the wayward peanut while William chuckled.

"Nesting is not your strong suit," William chided before tossing the seagull several peanuts, which it quickly swallowed. "Well, it's better than eating alone." The seagull offered no response as it jostled the last offered peanut before gulping it down. "Guess it's just you and me, you silly gull." The seagull chirped in reply, which surprisingly diminished William's loneliness. "So what do I call you?" William asked, not expecting an answer. The bird did not disappoint; it remained silent while cocking its head about as if taking in the scenery.

"Gully?" William asked. Again, no response from the bird. "Featherhead? Beaker?" Still silent, the bird now nipped at its feathers, ignoring the priest.

"Perch?" The seagull squawked loudly in response. "Perch it is," William said before tossing his companion another peanut. "Well, Perch, if there are any search craft out there, I need to set a fire to catch their attention. The mountainside offers the best chance to be seen, but climbing that mountain will drain me. Can you fly me up?" Perch said nothing as it returned to grooming its feathers.

"OK, so we walk," William said as he leaned down to the pond water and filled his now empty Pepsi bottle with water. Standing, William went through his clothes, washing each in the fresh water before hanging each from the branches of nearby poplar trees. Then, after donning one pair of chinos, a fresh-washed shirt and his deck shoes, William gathered his remaining possessions into his satchel and, with the saturated trench coat over his shoulder, began his climb up the mountain; the way was not easy.

The initial ascent required William to climb steep walls of granite that offered few footholds for the first twenty feet. Making it to the first ledge, William felt pride as if he surmounted Everest. His ego deflated the moment Perch glided in, landed at the priest's side and squawked.

"Showoff," William muttered as he fought to regain his breath. "Tell you what. Why don't you head up there and build a fire; I'll be right behind you." Perch remained silent as it started grooming feathers once more. Minutes turned to hours before William gathered the strength to carry onward. Without looking to check if Perch was following, the priest continued on picking the gentlest slopes to scale. Days without a substantial meal, his stomach chimed in repeatedly throughout the journey to the summit as William's mind bombarded him with memory of his favorite foods.

"A slice of Pasquale's pizza, some barbeque chicken wings and a large Pepsi would taste real good right about now," he said before taking a sip of water. "Or maybe a couple tacos from Ultima Taco. Mmm, tacos." William's stomach gurgled at the mention of his favorite food. A sudden chirp from Perch reminded William he was not alone. He turned to his avian companion and smiled. "Tell you what, you go pick up the food and I'll pay. Deal?" Without another sound, Perch took off and disappeared into the sun. "Don't forget the Pepsi!" Perch returned minutes later, landing at William's feet, a small fish in its mouth. The priest smiled.

"That ain't Pasquale's pizza."

***

The duo ate a light supper together, Perch eating the fish and William a bag of Doritos. Then, with renewed energy, they finished their ascent. The summit was a shelf of granite bifurcated by lines of feldspar and quartz. While vegetation was sparse, grasses and stunted conifers provided enough greenery to create a picturesque setting, which only grew in mystic and wonder. With the sun starting to dip into the horizon, its rays cast foreboding orange hues across the ocean's sea-blue palette.

"My God," Father William whispered. For a moment, the scene reminded him of sunrises off Acadia National Park. Two different summers he spent in the park on retreats while in the seminary. Every morning of the retreat he spent in solitude near Thunder Hole, watching the sunrise. For a time, he hoped to be assigned to a parish with a similar view. That thought brought clarity.

"I'm home."

Chapter 5

William gathered dried grass and twigs in the fading sunlight. With a wealth of fallen tree limbs scattered over the area, William had everything he needed for a bonfire, and he intended to avail himself of the opportunity. With the dried grass as tinder, William struck a fragment of granite with the satchel's metal clasp. After showering the grass with the subsequent sparks, he cupped his hands around the grass and blew softly into the mass; a flame took hold.

"Experimental archaeology in action," he said with pride. "College definitely paid off." After adding twigs and branches, the fire soon roared to life casting rivulets of flame up towards the stars. Once certain the fire was stabilized, William stood just beyond the firelight to scan the now cloudless sky for sign of searchers. As only a sliver of moon and faint starlight reined above, William knew his bonfire would easily catch the attention of pilots or ship captains. From his position on the mountain, he also reasoned he would spot the lights of aircraft and ships within miles of the island. Yet, all was dark beyond. If not for the audible crashing of the waves along the shore, William imagined he could have been standing on the edge of a bottomless ravine. He was certain no rescue was underway, as certain as he was that the beach rested below and not the Abyss.

Turning from his watch, William walked back into the firelight sitting well within the rim of warmth. After propping the trench coat up with sticks to help it dry, William sat on a slab of granite where he turned his attention to his few worldly possessions. His focus turned immediately to the black, vinyl case. Pulling open the zipper, William reached inside to grab his books, each in gallon-sized, zipper-topped bags. He hesitated, wondering if the seals held. Slowly retracting his hand, William became overwrought with joy. The seals of both bags remained clasped, undamaged. His books were dry. He received the first book, a pocket-sized Bible, at his First Communion, a gift from his parents. Removing the Bible from the protective bag, Father William opened to the inside where a bookplate read *"To our son on his 1st Communion. With Love, Mom and Dad."* William gently touched the handwriting as he smiled.

"Mom's handwriting," he said as Perch walked into view and settled into a patch of grass. "Her handwriting is the most beautiful I've ever seen. Much better than mine and Dad's for that matter. Dad would give any doctor a run for their money." Closing the cover, a sense of comfort took hold. His parents were with him. The second book, dry and intact, held a different significance.

"David and Leigh Eddings," William said aloud as he scanned the cover. "The Belgariad and Malloreon Collections, fantasy epics at their best." For a time, William thought over the stories within, stories he reread yearly since first coming across the Eddings' work during the 1990's while an undergrad. "You know, a lot more kids would be proficient readers if schools assigned fantasy classics like this," he said, holding the book out towards Perch; the seagull chirped in reply. "Well, if I'm gonna be stuck here for eternity, I can't think of two better works to have with me."

Thud-thud-thud! The sound came fast and from outside the sphere of firelight. Thud-thud-thud! Father William grabbed the Bible, holding it fast to his chest, and backed-up towards the fire.

Thud-thud thud! The sound drew closer.

"In the name of God, show yourself!" Father William exclaimed. With a single bound, a rabbit jumped into view. The rodent then scratched at its back with its hind leg, an action that generated the sound William feared. Falling to his knees, Father William simply shook his head in relief and disbelief.

"Bad rabbit," he said, waving a disapproving finger at his new guest who just continued scratching. William chuckled, the only response that seemed appropriate under the circumstances. With the crashing waves and crackling fire in the background, William felt imbedded in a Norman Rockwell moment. Yet with the presence of Perch and the rabbit, William reasoned Dr. Seuss was on the island pulling the strings.

Convinced no beasts lurked in the darkness waiting to devour him, William put a few more branches on the fire, grabbed the now dry trench coat and rested on a granite slab within the reach of the firelight. The night air warm, William used the coat as a pillow instead of as a blanket. Once comfortable, he said a prayer of thanksgiving before opening the Bible to read *The Book of Exodus*.

***

Thud-thud-thud! The rabbit's persistent kicking against a slab of granite jarred William from dreams of pizza, Pepsi and tacos.

"Is that really necessary?" William asked as his eyes adjusted to the growing sunlight. He positioned his hands over his eyes to shield them from the sunlight, making it possible to focus his vision.

One problem solved. Now William just needed to adjust to the headache piercing his sinuses.

"I need coffee," William said as he sat up. His joints, stiff and sore from sleeping on rock, made movement difficult, yet his collective aches were soon soothed by his now focused sight. Gazing out over the calm surf, William watched the aerial acrobatics of a flock of seagulls flying just above the waves in unison. Suddenly, the mass of birds climbed with small groups separating into new flight paths. One bird flew off alone, soaring high before diving towards William. Within seconds, the seagull landed at the priest's feet, a minnow in its mouth.

"Morning, Perch," William said. "Is that fish for me?" Perch ignored his friend, gulping down the fish before waddling to a nearby patch of grass. Once nestled in the green blades of grass, Perch started to groom its feathers. Turning back to his possessions, William collected his books and remaining foodstuffs into the satchel, leaving only his soggy journal behind. "That's going to need some time to dry," he said before placing the journal on a rock, the unused book opened to expedite drying.

Thud-thud-thud. The rabbit's persistence showed no sign of diminishing.

"Enough with the pounding, you silly rabbit!" Surprisingly, the rabbit ended its movements and just stared at William. "How did you even get up here?" William asked, not that the rabbit responded. Instead, the rabbit just turned and bounced away with Perch waddling behind.

"Follow the leader," William said before following his companions down the mountain.

Chapter 6

Perch abandoned the trek within a few feet, taking flight and gliding down the mountain.

"Showoff!" William exclaimed, feeling abandoned while sympathizing with the ground-challenged aviator. When he returned his attention to his guide, the rabbit was gone. "Rabbit? RABBIT?" William sprinted ahead looking for the long-eared rodent. Running into a clump of bushes, William found the rabbit's path down the mountain; it began with a sharp incline.

William fell forward and started rolling down the mountainside, audibly, and hit every rock and thorny bush for thirty feet. He regained composure and some pride just as the rabbit returned, its leg pounding on the ground. Thud-thud-thud!

"I'm just gonna call you Thud. Sound good?" The rabbit made no reply before turning and jumping further down the mountain.

***

Thud's route down the mountain proved a significant improvement over William's first path, at least after the first thirty feet. Once at the mountain's base, it took little time to reach the trees where his clothes were hanging.

"Well, I guess it's time to make a real shelter. The rain won't hold off forever," William said as he packed up his clothes. Scanning around, he considered different locations and shelter designs. "I guess I should've watched more Survivor episodes," he said while calculating his immediate needs. "Well, a lean-to would be a good start," William whispered as he bent over to collect a few large branches in the immediate vicinity. Using two poplar saplings spaced seven feet apart as a base, William rested a large, felled branch against each sapling. Using vines to secure the branches to the saplings at forty-five degree angles, he had his lean-to frame. The difficulty came when he looked for branches to complete the roof. As the thickness of available branches usually tapered along the tree limb's length, the ultimate construction of the roof left gaps that would fail to keep out rain and critters.

"Well, it's a start," William said before looking for thatching material. After sparsely covering the roof with pine branches, William looked to the available cornstalks for a final roof coating. The result of his construction lacked finesse, but he reasoned it would do for now. Shelter secured, William looked to his food stores.

"Don't have much choice, do I?" William asked himself as he surveyed the small cornfield and neighboring pond. The corn itself, a mix of small red, yellow and gray kernels on a thin ear, provided some assurances, but William wanted to find additional staples for what he initially assumed would be a short stay on the island. Peering into the pond, he watched small grey fish the size of rock bass swim amongst the seaweed and rocks, oblivious to William's presence. Here swam his next staple. Pulling a fresh branch off a poplar tree, the priest removed the leaves and thinner branches to create a fishing spear.

"I should've taken a class in flint knapping," William said while considering options for adding a point to his spear. Ultimately, William smashed a chunk of quartz against a granite slab, an action that created a fresh, sharp edge along the broken quartz. He then sat by his lean-to, whittling down the thinner end of the branch until he created a half-inch thick point.

"Now, for the hard part," William whispered as he entered the pond barefoot. For a moment, he looked over at his companions. *Would they leave once they watched William kill another animal?* That thought heavy on his mind, William stood and waited, not so patiently. Time passed and nothing swam near him. The first fish that did enter his area of the pond, nearly an hour after he started his hunt, was not much larger than a minnow. William did not even attempt to spear it. Minutes later, one of the gray fish, nearly ten inches in length, caught his eye.

"Come on. Come on," William whispered, an effort to egg on his dinner. It seemed to work; the fish swam closer. Ten feet... five feet... three feet...

William jabbed the spear into the water and missed his prey by ample inches. Frustrated, William ran after the fish, jabbing the spear into the water whenever he got close. Then, when he got within two feet of the fish, he slipped on a sand covered slab of granite and fell backwards into the pond.

"So this is why people become vegetarians?" William asked aloud. Propping his torso out of the water, he scanned the surface of the pond for evidence of fish breaching the surface. Instead of spotting more prey, he witnessed Perch fly to the pond's edge, wade into the shallows and grab a large minnow with ease. Perch then exited the pond and swallowed his meal.

"Showoff!"

After gaining his footing, William stood, his buttocks sore from striking the hidden stone. Looking over his sea-weed-covered pants and shirt, he felt silly. Then, tasting a piece of seaweed, William thought over his options once more as he spit out the bitter vegetation.

"God, please let me catch a fish."

***

After reclaiming his spear, William scanned the pond's surface for a better fishing spot. As the sun was near its zenith, the pond surface was warm. Consequently, William looked for shade. Two options were available. The nearest, shaded by a large poplar, proved too deep for William to work in. The second, while in the shallows, presented a different dilemma; it was cluttered with reeds that resembled cattails.

'A weir!" William exclaimed, reasoning the reeds could work like a Native American fish trap that diverted fish towards shallow and confined spaces, which made it easier to spear them. He headed over to the reeds, anticipating better luck, and a school of fish fled the safety of the shade. Flustered, William positioned himself amidst the reeds and waited. Within little time, a number of fish returned and entrapped themselves in the circuitous mishmash of reeds, seaweed and ferns. The spear fishing went a lot easier at that point; William secured two in less than thirty minutes, the only difficulty being in killing the fish.

"God, forgive me and bless this fish," William said after killing each of his catches. He would repeat those words throughout the remainder of his life after each catch, the killing never getting easier.

Chapter 7

With the fish spitted on the spear and his impromptu water bottle refilled, William began his ascent up the mountain, reaching his previous mountaintop camp shortly before nightfall, Perch and Thud in tow. Again, he managed to start a fire with little trouble, and the flames reached good heights just as night took firm hold of the sky. In the firelight, William cleaned the two fish after which he secured the meat to two sticks he then held over the flames. His stomach growling throughout the process, William eagerly awaited the meal. Once the fish appeared appropriately singed, William placed the cooked meat on a rock to cool. Perch, appearing to have lost patience, waddled over to the fish to inspect.

"Hold on!" William exclaimed, blocking Perch's advance with his right hand. The priest then said his meal prayer before ripping off a piece of meat and throwing it to Perch, who eagerly gobbled the offered fare. The bird unceremoniously regurgitated the fish bits and walked away.

"Wait a minute. You'll eat garbage that's been rotting in the sun for months, but you won't eat my cooking? I'll have you know I have almost ten years of cooking experience at the Gardenview Restaurant, and no one ever complained about my cooking!" Perch moved off into the shadows without another sound. "Ingrate!"

William then tasted a piece of the fish for himself, and likewise spit it out.

"OK, good call." Then, as William returned to his vigil over dinner and wondered how to make the meal palatable, Thud bounced out of the woods, resting several feet from where William worked. The priest considered the approach of the rodent for a moment before tossing a bit of fish to Thud. After sniffing at the fish bit for several seconds, Thud gobbled up the offered meat. William half expected the rabbit to say *"please Sir, may I have some more."* The priest considered the ramifications of the rabbit's actions.

"I thought you were a vegetarian? You aren't related to the rabbit from Monty Python's *Holy Grail* are you?" The rabbit said nothing. "Great! I survived shark-infested waters only to end up lunch for a crazed rabbit." Thud turned and jumped into a patch of grass to feast, oblivious to the quip.

The meal was bland, but it satisfied William's hunger for the time. As with the previous night, William gazed out into the dark in search of rescue craft. Again, he spotted no lights, though he was not surprised.

"I wonder if anyone even knows this island exists?" William asked aloud before turning to where Perch rested in the grass. "If they do know of the island, I wonder if they think the fire is the work of a dragon?" William chuckled at the thought.

"So, it's the Lonely Mountain I have found, and Smaug has risen from his cave seeking the Hobbit thief that disturbed his sleep." A distant howl carried in the air wrestling the priest from his dream.

"And me without a wizard or dwarves for backup," William whispered as he pulled his spear close.

***

"No telling what's still out there, why tempt Fate," William said as he flung the remains of his meal over the mountain's steep wall. The howling still fresh in his ears, he did not want to take chances. After tossing a few more logs onto the fire, William settled down once more by the fire for reading light. Additionally, as the air had cooled significantly compared to the previous evening's hours, William gained the comfort of warmth the fire bestowed. Starting again with the Old Testament, Father William found he opened to verses referencing Jeroboam II of Israel, which ultimately led to mention of the prophet Jonah. Father William considered the prophet's journey in the whale's belly and the prophet's hesitation to serve.

"Is that why I'm here?" William asked, his head peering skyward. William feared the changes he faced. Yet, he long sought to serve Humanity in some way. Tomorrow would be his third day, and he had yet to serve in any capacity. Father William stayed awake for hours contemplating his failing to reach the mission in South America. As difficult as it was to leave his family, William reasoned this to be a great way to serve. "Now what will I do?" he asked. His companions, now nestled into one of his shirts, did not stir to remark in any manner to William's question. He knew he needed to find his own answer, without help, and William determined to find the answer in the morning.

***

Father William awoke to brilliant sunrays and the rhythmic call of the surf. Squinting, he slowly adjusted to the searing illumination punctuated by a shadow high overhead. Gradually, the shadow took shape, feathered wings and tail the first dimensions to draw clear. It was no seagull, of that William was certain, but a bird nevertheless. Its body shimmered in the light, radiating a luminescence like a full moon, and for long moments, the bird gently rode on the current of a warm breeze that touched even Father William.

A bitter howl emanating from the beach below shattered the silence carrying the bird above.

William was up in an instant, spear in hand. Sprinting to the summit's edge, the priest scanned about for the source of the howl, but he saw no predator below. The howl called again, and again William saw nothing save the birds flittering about the island. Thud and Perch wrestled out of their makeshift bed, which startled William. In an instant, the priest turned and raised his spear into a lancing stance, the spear's point aimed at the rabbit, which bounded out towards William.

"Ah!" he exclaimed, his heart pounding to the beat of his fear. "Oh

Thud, I'm sorry," he said, turning the spear from where his companion now sat. Thud seemed to take everything in stride, flinching only to grab a large blade of grass the rabbit then inhaled. The howl rose again into the air, and this time both Perch and Thud joined William in twisting about to pinpoint the source of the horrific bellow.

"I will not live in fear," William declared, as he marched to Thud's path to seek the Island's hidden monster. Perch and Thud followed close behind.

***

William kept a careful pace as he maneuvered down the mountainside. The spear readied for combat, he kept a careful eye to his periphery believing the monster was already stalking him. Additional howls carried in the air as William's trek progressed, each louder and more daunting than the last. Dashing amidst the maze of trees and island brush, William calculated possible beasts he might encounter, and every creature that came to mind terrified him.

His contemplation of the coming encounter ended the moment he heard the wail.

Father William stopped abruptly, contemplating the pain-choked wail now drowning out all other sounds. Did the monster have its prey? William bolted towards the beach intent on saving the monster's victim. Breaking through the last barrier of vegetation before the beach, William encountered the growling creature, which was more victim than predator.

Shrouded in a large, nylon fishing net, struggled a bull, elephant seal. Its body and proboscis strangled by the netting, William knew the creature's calls were not for warnings, but for help.

"It's OK, I can help you," William said, his voice just above a whisper. He edged closer to the seal, moving slowly with his palms raised. "It's going to be…"

The cry of two yellow-headed vultures overhead broke the passivity in the moment, rattling both the seal and the priest. The seal ignored the priest and turned to growl at its avian tormentors. The seal's action only tightened the grip of the netting causing the restrained seal to collapse into the surf. It was then that William spotted deep cuts to the seal's body, tears from the netting. He also knew the seal was exhausted the minute one of the vultures flew to the giant mammals back and dug deep into a wound; the seal growled but barely moved in defense. William acted, charging towards the seal and shooing away the bird with his spear. The vulture hissed as it elevated itself just out of the spear's reach.

"Get outta here!" William exclaimed. The seal remained still, undisturbed by the human's rant while the vulture hissed again, seemingly unimpressed. To the vulture's chagrin, Father William was not alone. Perch appeared as if out of nowhere and raked the vulture's back with his webbed feet. Amidst a flurry of shredded vulture feathers, the yellow-headed scavenger took flight with its companion close behind. Perch gave chase for nearly one hundred feet before turning back and circling overhead to provide cover. William beamed with hope and delight at his friend's actions, but the gravity of the situation came crashing back to reality with a thrust of the seal's caudal fin, which sent William flying into the sand.

The priest rose from sand clutching his left calf. Spitting out a mouthful of sand, grit and shell, he kept his distance from the seal assessing the best way to remove the net.

"We'll get you out of there," William said as he limped toward the seal. Inching forward, the seal showed no fear, which gave William the courage to reach out and rest his hand on the mammal's back. The seal remained near motionless, its breathing shallow and irregular. "I'll be right back," William said as he gently rubbed the seal's side. Then, slowly backing away, William moved off in search of a fragment of quartz or granite, which was not difficult to find. Smashing a fist-sized fragment of granite against a large slab of the rock, he exposed a new, razor sharp edge keen for slicing the netting. After cautiously returning to the ensnared elephant seal's side, William began slicing the netting, section by section, until the seal was free. Yet freedom failed to encourage the seal to seek the safety of the waves. Instead, the injured beast turned and examined William with great intent. Again, William rested his hand on the seal. The seal's breathing grew stronger with each breath, its pulse stronger.

"Go, my friend," William said as his brown eyes peered into the opaque eyes of the seal. Man and seal, mammal and mammal, the two felt connected in peace and trust. It was a feeling neither would ever forget. The seal leaned in towards the priest, nudging the man's shoulder with its head. Then, certain it relayed its gratitude, the elephant seal bounded towards the water to search for nourishment, healing and freedom.

"Live well," William whispered, his eyes locked on the water plume left in the seal's wake. "Now this is a mission I could get used to."

Chapter 8

William sat in the surf for a time, allowing the incoming tide to wash over him. Yards behind him, safely beyond the water's reach, Perch and Thud waited patiently, the gull cleaning its feathers and the rabbit eating ferns. Far from the snow and cold of Buffalo, William now sat in the warm, salty waters of a new home, a new parish. Watching for signs of the elephant seal or the pod of dolphins that rescued him, William considered the calm within him and a renewed sense of contentment and purpose, which long eluded him since the closing of his childhood parish; St. Bonaventure Parish of West Seneca. There, against the backdrop of ruffled waves and the cry of marine birds, William realized the perfect name for his sanctuary; the Island Parish of St. Bonaventure.

"It's good to be home," William said, contented. A break in the mounting cloud cover unleashed a steady beam of sunlight, which warmed Father William to the bone while simultaneously elucidating an object caught by the rising surf. The priest raised his hands to his forehead, an attempt to hold back the strain of the sunlight. He could just barely make out the object, which seemed at the mercy of the ocean waves. He stood and strode towards it, mesmerized by the object's chameleon act, one minute appearing as an oblong crystal, the next as a lusterless bottle well hidden amidst the churning tide. The current steady, the object soon floated within reach, and Father William did not hesitate to free the object from the water. It was an empty, plastic water bottle. The label of the twenty-ounce bottle weathered, he could only discern the words 'filtered water.' The bottle was a momentary disturbance of his sanctuary causing William to scan the horizon for a ship or boat that littered the seas with the plastic refuse. He beheld nothing but calm waters beyond the chaos of the tide. Looking over the bottle once more, William did not fail to note the hypocrisy of the label's small print asking consumers to "please recycle" when there were no receptacles available on the island or in most urban areas.

"At least I can help clean the oceans," William said as he walked back beyond the surf's reach. Sitting by Perch, resting the bottle of the ground, William returned to his meditations. Never before had he felt such peace, so alive.

"I wish I could share this with the world," he said. Not a second later, a breeze picked up, blowing the plastic bottle to William's side. He smiled.

"Maybe I *can* share this place with the world," William said, lifting and holding up the bottle to the sun. "Come on, Perch. We've got work to do."

***

With the spear in one hand and the bottle in the other, William marched towards the pond. Perch and Thud followed close behind. After rinsing out the bottle, William maneuvered over to the reeds to catch lunch. William waited twenty minutes, motionless, before a

large, grass carp moved into the confined space; one strike of the spear
caught the carp. Grabbing two ears of
corn, the bottle and the carp, William
headed to the mountain path at a steady
pace and reached the summit in half an
hour with Thud bouncing along behind
and Perch circling overhead.

"We don't have much time," William said aloud as he cleaned and spitted
the carp before starting a small, cooking
fire. Fueling the growing fire with sticks
and dried grass, William soon had a sufficient amount of ash and coals in which
he placed the ears of corn. Then, while
his meal cooked, he prepared and ignited
the bonfire pit, gathering sufficient wood
to fuel the fire well into the night. The
fire stabilized, he then placed the plastic
bottle near the fire to expedite its drying.

"Almost ready," he said turning to
retrieve his meal. After saying grace,
William consumed the carp while the
corn cooled on a granite slab. "Well, it's
at least tastier than the other fish." Perch
curiously examined the corn, but seemed
uninterested in the vegetable. However,

the bird eagerly swallowed the bits of carp William tossed on the ground at the bird's webbed feet. Thud, meanwhile, ignored the fish bits and focused on grass and ferns for nourishment.

"Not the carnivore I thought you were, Thud," William said, smiling as Thud munched down a thick blade of grass. The rabbit's eyes stared back at the priest, reflecting a total lack of malice. "Guess I don't have to worry about waking up with my ears gnawed off." William smiled at the sight of his would-be congregation. The rabbit and the bird were not gregarious companions, but their presence brought solace. "Here's to silent but faithful friends," William said raising his bottle of water to toast the gull and the hare. William spent the remainder of his meal in silence, eating one ear of corn while scraping the kernels off the other for Thud and Perch, the latter of which consumed only a few kernels. Dinner finished, William set to his plan.

"It's time," William said as he packed up his belongings before piling

more wood on the growing bonfire.
Without another word, he began his
march back down the mountain in the
waning sunlight.

***

So it was on the third day, Father
William Sullivan said his first Mass.
First blessing the pond and its water, Father William proceeded to dunk a nee-
dle-rich pine branch into the freshwater
and then shake the Holy Water over the
lean-to and the ground upon which the
structure rested. Here he would ultimately erect a new St. Bonaventure
Church. While he would never have
human parishioners to serve, each Mass
he celebrated would have attendees;
Perch, Thud and other creatures intrigued by the priest's homilies and sing-
ing. On this day, he focused his homily
on reaching out towards others and
providing hope where none existed previously.

"Our words, our actions, can bring peace and comfort to those most in need," Father William said, his voice booming over the sound of the surf. "We need only take time out of our busy lives to bring forth the hope we all desperately need." Those words resonated through Father William's thoughts while he continued the Mass, every word and verse only accentuating his call to action. After completing the Mass, Father William, draped in the rescued trench coat and his rosary hanging from his neck, led a processional to where his possessions rested. Squatting down to the sand, he reached into his satchel and removed his now dry journal. In the waning sunlight, William thought of people and actions that made a difference in his life and wrote each thought down. Then, considering the list he generated, he ripped out a fragment of paper and wrote down a message. William folded the scrap of paper and stuffed it into the bottle he recovered from the ocean.

"And so it begins," he said, considering the new mission he had accepted. With Perch and Thud in tow, Father William walked to the beach to watch the sun complete its plunge into the distant horizon. With thoughts of his family, William removed the rock he used as a small knife and carved his initials into the bottle's cap. Then, with the tide receding and the sun releasing its last tendrils of daylight, he cast the bottle back into the sea.

"Please God, may this message bring hope to who needs it most."

Chapter 9

Dillon sat patiently, waiting for his time with a career center counselor while other students, equally lost, flipped through magazines and pamphlets from the center's reference library, hoping to find direction for the future. In truth, Dillon questioned going to the center. What point would it serve? Friends had praised the career center's staff for being encouraging and skilled at helping students uncertain of which major or career was a good fit to their respective interests. Identifying his interests had never been a problem for Dillon. Explaining his interests to his mother, on the other hand, had been difficult if not impossible.

"Dillon?" called out a student assistant who escorted the brown haired, twenty year old into an office stocked with books, run of the mill office furniture and a career counselor eager to *help* Dillon move forward. The meeting went as expected. Dillon looked into the counselor's blue eyes and listened intently as the light-brown haired woman summarized the results of the Strong Interest Inventory he completed two weeks prior. As a biology major headed towards medical school, Dillon's family, friends and professors would expect the results of the career assessment to indicate that Dillon's interests matched well with physicians, lab techs, pharmacists, and researchers. Yet, Dillon knew better, as did the career counselor.

"Your interests and aptitude lean heavily toward the arts, Dillon. Between the inventory's results and your folder, I'm surprised you aren't pursuing a fine arts degree." He looked at the cover she referred to, a two-pocket portfolio with a flawless, hand-drawn rendition of the University's mascot; a bull. Yet, unlike the design pictured on team uniforms and student apparel, Dillon's depiction was of a full-bodied beast with muscle tone that would put any body-builder to shame.

"Dillon, are you all right?" The counselor asked after moments of silence passed without him saying anything.

"I'm fine. I appreciate your time," he said before bolting from the center to wander the campus in search of direction and comfort.

For two years now, South Florida University had been Dillon's home. Living close by, he commuted for classes. However, finding work as a lab assistant and biology tutor, he spent most of each day on campus, essentially staying at his childhood home just long enough to sleep and shower. It was not that he loved being on campus, Dillon simply wanted as much time to immerse himself in biology-related organizations as possible, hoping to find direction towards a focus in biology that would grab him. He attended lectures, tours of local laboratories and even field trips to preserves hoping that each would show him a side of biology worth *doing* everyday. Two years passed and still nothing in biology peaked his interest. What did, however, were drawing and painting. After meeting with doctors and researchers, Dillon spent hours drawing portraits of the individuals whose work intrigued him. Likewise, any trip into the field took Dillon to natural settings he could not help but record in pencil or paint during or after the trips. The movement of pencil and brush calmed Dillon, making him feel whole in a way the sciences never did.

After the meeting with the career center counselor, Dillon sat in the commuter lounge while generating a pencil sketch of the woman. Her words of encouragement brought some solace where his mother's words brought grief.

"There are NO jobs for artists; that's why they starve!" Dillon's mother exclaimed anytime he mentioned a career in art. "You are throwing away all my hard work getting you through school. I am not paying thousands of dollars a semester for you to play with crayons and paint! Waste your own money."

"Maybe she's right," Dillon kept telling himself until he ultimately registered as a biology major, which appeased his mother. A paralegal, Dillon's mother had worked hard up the ladder, starting as a receptionist until finally putting herself through college to be able to assist lawyers with court cases. He knew she wanted Dillon to have an easier life, which was part of the reason he bent to her will. His father was another story entirely.

Attending a community college, Dillon's father completed an associate's degree in hotel management before opening his automotive repair shop just south of Tampa. His father worked exclusively on classics, which were abundant throughout Florida. Everyday Dillon's father came home exhausted and covered in oil, grease and blood. Then after eating dinner and spending time with his family, Dillon's father retreated to his workshop in the garage. There, Dillon's father built music boxes, clocks and an assortment of items, both functional and decorative, for friends and family. To Dillon, it seemed as if his father never stopped working for others.

"She just wants what's best for me," Dillon said as he finished the drawing.

Now the lone occupant of the commuter lounge, Dillon put aside his drawing pad before meandering through the chairs, tables and benches to reach the vending machines. With just five dollars on hand, he settled for an egg salad sandwich on wheat bread and a bottle of Dr. Pepper for dinner. Then, sitting near a large, bay window, Dillon ate his meal while watching the sunset and contemplating a life invested in science. The solitude and scenery failed to bring serenity.

Grabbing a late bus home, Dillon continued his thoughts about his career choices and current class load; all science and no art. "How would this path bring contentment?" he asked himself while making the final leg of his journey home. Walking up the sidewalk to his family's front door, Dillon still found no answer.

"Dammit!" exclaimed a voice from the garage, which woke Dillon from his stupor. Dillon made his way over to the garage's side door, intent on finding out what irked his father this time.

"Dad, you ok?" Dillon asked as he peered in through the door.

"Yeah, just mistook my thumb for a nail, is all," replied his father who stood over his workbench while shaking his right hand.

"I'm surprised you have any thumbs or fingers left," Dillon said as he set his books and pad down on a vacant tabletop and sat on one of the stools his father made. The creaking of the maple stool settled quickly but not before Dillon reconsidered sitting.

"It's safe," his father said before returning to the project at hand.

"What are you working on this time?" Dillon asked as he stretched his neck in an effort to see over his father's stout shoulders. If not for their similar hair, eye color and facial features, one would never guess they were father and son. Dillon was tall and thin, like a blade of grass that the Florida winds tossed about at will. His father, meanwhile, was several inches shorter, but built like a brick wall that winds failed to ruffle.

"A display case for your mother; she wanted something to display those figurines she gets with her tea. Would you grab me a soda from the fridge?"

"Sure," Dillon replied before walking over to the small fridge his father kept stocked in the garage. After opening the fridge's door, Dillon grabbed two cans of birch beer before heading back to his father's workbench. Setting down the drinks on the bench, Dillon looked on as his father finished sanding the small case's main shelf. Built of slender oak planks, the case needed no staining as the wood's grain and coloring seemed perfectly matched throughout.

"Not bad, huh?" his father asked before opening one of the cans of birch beer. Dillon did not reply. Instead, he reached out and felt the sanded wood, which felt as if his father had already applied a protective resin.

"It's beautiful." Dillon's tone spoke volumes.

"What's wrong, Dill?" his father asked while cleaning off a file with a wire brush. "Math again?"

"I'll get it, eventually," Dillon replied as he recalled his recent Calculus quiz grade, a 57%.

"If you're not happy, pursue something else. It's as simple as that," remarked his father as the would-be carpenter blew sawdust off the file. For Dillon, it was not so simple.

"I just don't see much opportunity for artists, at least not enough for raising a family."

"That's your mother talking, Dill. Sooner or later, you are gonna have to determine what's best for you," his father said as he picked up another file to clean.

"I don't want to disappoint her or you," Dillon replied, words that drew a stern look from his father.

"Dill, I don't care what you do or what degree you pursue. You want to be a doctor? Fine. You want to be an artist? That's fine, too. What matters to me is that you're happy in the path you've chosen. No matter what, you will face challenges and defeats down the road. The question is, when tough times arise, do you want to be following your dream or someone else's?"

***

Dillon was up early the next morning to attend a service-learning field trip with his environmental biology class. The class was to assist with clean up efforts at a stretch of beach along McKay Bay. Equipped with hip waders, a litterbag and a trash stick, Dillon and his classmates scoured the beach in search of food wrappers, bottles and other trash that could injure or contaminate inhabitants of the area. While he was eager to assist with the effort, Dillon could not help thinking about his future.

"What path should I take?" he asked himself continually while considering both the draw of medicine and his love of art. Dillon also spent time debating feedback from his mother, professors and father. "What path should I take?"

The cry of a seagull abruptly ended his concentration and diverted his attention to a clump of trash floating twenty feet away from the beach; a seagull waddled across the surface of the trash heap continually calling out in unintelligibe chirps and whines. Dillon went to work.

Wadding into the surf, he slowly approached the bird and its little island. When he was within arm's length of the bird, it flew off into the sun. Squinting, Dillon watched with delight as the bird looped about in the sky before disappearing into the searing sunlight. Smiling, Dillon began pulling the floating pile of trash into his litterbag until he came across a plastic soda bottle with a folded piece of paper inside. He lifted the bottle to get a better look and noticed handwriting, but the folded layers made it impossible to read. Then, after gathering the remaining refuse, Dillon walked back to the beach where he removed his gloves, the bottle's cap, and the message inside. Expecting a limerick, pun, or dirty joke, Dillon found something entirely different.

"A father's wisdom will lead us to the right path," Dillon said as he read the message, stunned by its implications.

Smiling, Dillon felt a great weight lifted off his heart. That evening, Dillon submitted a portfolio of his best drawings and paintings, beginning the declaration process for the university's Bachelor of Fine Arts in Studio Arts. His application was accepted.

Dillon's remaining two years of coursework at the university allowed him to explore new techniques in drawing and painting. Traveling the coastal areas, Dillon employed his new knowledge in creating oil, watercolor, and charcoal renderings depicting Florida's rich landscapes, pieces that garnered considerable attention when displayed at local galleries statewide. Upon graduation, he obtained a position as an illustrator for an advertising firm, work that offered opportunities for Dillon to illustrate magazines, newspaper copy, websites, and, to his mother's delight, medical texts. Ultimately, Dillon refocused his efforts on his landscape paintings, traveling the country to capture picturesque scenery in oils, chalk, watercolors and graphite. In time, he developed an art school where he trained a generation of landscape artists while advocating increased availability of funding towards the arts in museums and schools. Asked near the end of his long life what made him decide to make art the core of his life, he simply remarked, "I listened to my father and my heart."

Chapter 10

The stale air reeked of pipe tobacco, leather and old paper, a perfect melding of library and a centuries-old mansion. It was everything Maria expected the Smith, Douglas and Associates law firm to be.

"Ms. Angeles?" called out the receptionist, pulling Maria from her thoughts. "The partners will see you now." Without hesitation, Maria rose from her leather-shrouded chair and marched towards the receptionist, her leather briefcase in hand. Standing a towering six feet, Maria's trim, fit build and long, brown hair projected the march of a model down a runway. Yet, her green eyes cut through that illusion. To the honest, Maria's eyes beaconed hoped. To the corrupt, those same eyes cast forth terror and an impending sense of doom. Maria Angeles was the litigator that every version of Law and Order attempted to capture, and Smith and Douglas sought to snag the new Harvard graduate before any other firm did.

The receptionist escorted Maria down a long hallway to a conference room bordered by dark stained bookcases and portraits of America's founders wherever space allowed. At the room's heart rested a grand Kittinger mahogany conference table, and seated along the length of one side sat three women.

"Welcome, Ms. Angeles," said the woman seated in the center chair. "Please be seated." Maria sat in the chair directly opposing the partner who spoke. Maria, unaccustomed to timidity, struggled to respond to the partner. The gathered partners looked like twins, all middle-aged with long, blond hair and piercing blue eyes. They reminded Maria of the 'Stepford Wives,' an image enhanced by the fact each wore somewhat-matching navy pantsuits.

"Thank you for coming in today, Ms. Angeles," the middle woman said, pulling Maria from her thoughts. "I am Elisabeth Smith, senior partner, and this is our managing partner Michelle Douglas and our chief litigator, Renee Osborne," she said nodding to the women respectively.

"It's a pleasure to meet you all," Maria replied, nodding back to each. "I appreciate your inviting me here."

"It was our pleasure, Ms. Angeles," the senior partner said before flipping through pages in the folder before her. "You're a hot commodity, Maria. Harvard graduate, top of your class, bilingual, and you spent two summers as a law clerk in Judge Reynolds' office; quite impressive."

"It's been an incredible journey the last couple years," Maria replied, grateful that the senior partner missed none of her major accomplishments; Maria never felt comfortable tooting her own horn.

"Judge Reynolds hears a lot of environmental and medical malpractice cases, correct?" the managing partner asked, as if a switch just turned her on. The woman's tone was cold and sharp.

"Yes," Maria replied. "I spent an equal time between both types of cases."

"And what of the bar exams?" Ms. Osborne asked, interjecting before Ms.

Douglas could continue her line of questioning.

"I've taken both the New York and Massachusetts bar exams, but I haven't received the results yet."

"That's ok," Ms. Osborne said. "We received your results yesterday. You scored within the top five percent on each bar, making you eligible to practice immediately." Maria found it difficult to gather breath for a moment as the enormity of the news confused her emotions. She wanted to scream, rejoice, but Maria also wanted to remain calm, poised, as if she expected to pass both exams.

"I had not anticipated receiving the news until next week. I appreciate your informing me," Maria said, hoping she concealed her pride and jubilation.

"Ms. Angeles," continued Ms. Smith. "We handle a lot of medical malpractice through our New York office as well as here in Boston. With your obvious talent and varied experience, we'd like to bring you in as an associate. Are you interested? Your starting salary would be one hundred thousand dollars. We would also set you up initially in an apartment near the office until you found a place of your own." Just as she had regained her composure and ability to breathe, Maria felt broadsided again; she expected to start out with a salary significantly less than that offered. Stunned, she remained silent.

"Are you all right, Maria?" asked Ms. Osborne.

"I'm fine, just a little surprised. The salary is quite generous, to say the least. However, I thought I was being considered for your environmental branch?" The partners glanced at one another, obviously rattled.

"We are now covering more medical cases and planning to phase out our environmental division within five years," Ms. Douglas said. "We've signed on to defend some major clients in the coming months, which will be a great opportunity for you to make your mark." Maria, long interested in environmental law, particularly in defending actions that preserved wetlands, felt betrayed. The discussions she had with the firm's headhunter never brought to light the move towards a strictly medical malpractice clientele. The senior partner pushed the conversation forward in an attempt to distract Maria from the obvious deception.

"The market is stocked with environmental attorneys, Maria, but fewer cases are coming to light," Ms. Smith said. "That's part of the reason we're making the change. Do you want to end up like one of a thousand environmentalists now working as an assistant D.A. or in some small, unknown firm struggling to find clients? The environment has a lot of protections in place. Meanwhile, doctors and pharmaceutical companies are inundated with false accusations from people looking for a quick buck. This is where you can make a significant impact. Not just in helping clear court dockets of sham lawsuits, but in potentially steering future legislation."

"This could be a start towards a storied career," Ms. Osborne added. "Why don't you take the weekend to consider

our offer; we know it's a big decision."
Maria felt that was the biggest under-
statement she ever heard.

***

"So, this is where freedom took
some of its first steps," Maria said as she
looked down to the rock whose surface
was unblemished save for the number
'1620' chiseled into it. "Plymouth
Rock." A day after her meeting in Boston at Smith, Douglas and Associates,
Maria was no closer to making her decision. Standing on the shelter built over
the relocated rock made famous by the
Pilgrim's landing, Maria considered the
importance of the historic site while
simultaneously debating the pros and
cons of the job offer. The money and
prestige were significant, to say the least.
Yet, what she most wanted was to pursue environmental litigation, protecting
the environment while also supporting
development that was necessary or bene-
ficial to society without negatively impacting natural resources. Resting her

hand on the stone edifice protecting the monumental rock, Maria felt a moment of peace. About her, people walked by without glancing at the historical structure.

"I wonder how many even know this is here?" she asked aloud, upset that she spent two years at Harvard University and only now made her way to Plymouth. Casting aside her personal chastisement, Maria walked to the nearby beach, which skirted Plymouth Bay. Instead of heading toward the Mayflower II, Maria walked in the opposite direction to distance herself from the docked ships and the flurry of people about the sea craft. The walk allowed Maria to smell the cool, salt-laden air coming off the bay. A seagull, which landed just a few yards down the beach, squawked loudly drawing Maria's attention.

"My God, these things are everywhere," Maria chided, as she continued her trek down the beach after circumnavigating the bird; the bird waited a few moments before waddling behind in pursuit. The trek of the lawyer and the gull ended a short distance later, their path obstructed by a woman staring at vials of water.

"Conducting an experiment?" Maria asked as she approached the young, red-haired woman.

"Nothing to see here, the sights are north of here," the woman replied in a dismissing tone before using an eyedropper to insert a violet dye into one of the vials. She then went on staring at the water.

"One of the most significant areas in American history, and you're looking at the water?" Maria asked, now very intrigued.

"Believe me, the water is very much a part of America's history, or at least it will be," the woman replied as she knelt down and set the vials into a black case that reminded Maria of her father's tackle box.

"What are you looking for? Bacteria?" Maria asked. The woman looked up and seemed to consider Maria's question.

"Not bacteria, but chemicals. There's a company down the coast that says its production activities and waste disposal are not impacting the water. I'm just gathering evidence that they're wrong."

"Were you hired by an attorney to test the water?" Maria asked as she walked closer.

"I am the attorney on the case," the woman said as she collected her equipment.

"You should really have an outside group take the samples; judges take neutral sources more seriously," Maria said as she looked out towards the water.

"Let me guess, you're a law student?" The woman asked rhetorically.

"No, I'm a lawyer who's completed a lot of environmental impact studies; just trying to give some friendly advice."

"Let me guess again, you're a Harvard grad?" Maria nodded in reply. "Well, *Harvard*, I had an independent source as well as a partner, and both were then hired away by the company I'm investigating. I didn't have much choice seeing as the hearing is tomorrow. If you're interested, I'm looking for a new partner." Maria laughed.

"You sure they were hired by the company and it wasn't your charm that chased them away?" The woman stood toe to toe with Maria who simply smirked. "Let me guess, Yale?" The woman nodded.

"Michelle Winslow," she said extending her hand, which Maria shook.

"I'm just going to call you, *Yale*," Maria said nonchalantly. "I'm Maria Angeles. So, how much you pay your partners?"

"Well, since you're from *Harvard*, you'll first have to start off as an associate," Michelle responded smartly. "My partner was making $50,000 a year, so, I'll hire you at $40,000. If you're interested, just meet me at the Plymouth courthouse tomorrow at 10:00 am." Without another word, Michelle moved off towards Plymouth Rock. Maria, in awe at the meeting, looked out at the water hoping Michelle would be successful. Then, lost in thoughts of her respective job offers, one serious and one not so much, Maria was brought back to reality by the squawking of the seagull. Looking down towards the water, she saw the seagull retreating from a bottle carried to shore by the rising tide, a bottle that was not empty. Pulling the glass, cork-capped bottle from the surf, Maria looked within; a curled up message rested inside. After removing the cork, Maria shook the message out and opened it revealing its message: *"Happiness and contentment are not in the money we attain, but in the causes we champion."*

***

Michelle Winslow pulled her aging Subaru into a courthouse parking space minutes before 10:00 am. Hurriedly, she pulled together her notes and briefcase and sprinted towards the courthouse, where Maria waited.

"Good morning, *Harvard,*" Michelle said as she reached the doorway where Maria waited. "Did you lose your way?"

"Not really, *Yale*. I just thought I'd stop by and make sure you didn't screw things up. Come on. Let's go defend *America's Hometown*." The two smiled and entered the courthouse. They fought the good fight, winning the court case while also forging a solid partnership, which they would maintain for decades as *Winslow and Angeles Associates*.

Chapter 11

"What am I going to do now?" Alicia asked as she pulled into her driveway, her tired, gray Escort wagon struggling to make it all the way into her garage. Shutting off the engine, she waited as the engine coughed to a full stop. With a click of the garage door remote, Alicia was corralled into one of the last places where she felt she had control. Exhausted and scared, she rested her forehead on the steering wheel, her long, auburn hair shrouding her whole head and muffling her sobs. After a time, her tears somewhat controlled, she exited her car and retrieved a box from her backseat before entering the connecting house.

A light-blue ranch, with a wood burning fireplace and a small backyard, the house was Alicia's 1200 square foot dream, a dream she worried she would now lose.

"What am I going to do now?" she asked herself again as she placed the box containing the contents of her desk onto

the kitchen table. She then walked into
the living room and curled up on the fu-
ton she had from her college years.
Drained after a day of mixed emotions,
fear and nausea, Alicia drifted asleep
thinking of how she would pay her
mortgage now that she was unemployed.

***

The first morning was the hardest,
though days did not get much better af-
terwards. Alicia was at a loss. With a
degree in museum studies, she planned
to find work as a curator for a historical
society or a science museum, but the
economy had different plans. With the
Great Recession occurring months before her graduation, museums, usually
the first to face a loss of financial support, started laying off employees in
droves. Desperate for a job, Alicia took
a fulltime position at the Charleston
bank where she had worked while an
undergraduate. Her plan was to work as
a teller until a museum job opened. After four years of not finding a curator

position, Alicia settled in at the bank, accepting an assistant manager position that offered a modest raise and more job security. Two years later, having saved for a down payment, she purchased a small home not far from the bank. While small, the house provided her with a sense of stability. Now, without a job, she worried she would lose that house just as she lost her job and benefits.

"What do I do now?" she asked herself each morning. "What if I get sick? What if the house needs a major repair? What is I can't afford to pay for food?" The questions she considered daily were endless, each bringing a separate set of desperate scenarios that she dreaded to contemplate. Immediately after her bank closed, she downsized. She canceled cable television and her landline, relying solely on her cell phone for contacting people. Additionally, she used her car sparingly to save on gas. Yet, with all the sacrifices she made, Alicia still had an uphill battle given her mortgage and monthly utilities.

As for finding a new job, that was Alicia's new job. She looked through local newspapers and on the internet for job openings and applied for every position she felt qualified for including bank teller, administrative assistant, housekeeping and cashier positions. After a month of submitting résumés and cover letters, she received not a single response. Scared and weary, Alicia's health deteriorated. She struggled to eat and sleep, which made it difficult to focus on anything; depression set in and hope vanished.

One month turned to three months, and Alicia's small reserve of savings were nearly exhausted. Emaciated, she found it hard to get up in the morning and even harder to keep down any food.

"What did I do wrong?" she asked herself. Embarrassed by not finding a museum position and by losing her bank job, Alicia could not bring herself to tell anyone she lost her job. "How do I explain my failure? What if my family is ashamed of me?" Those questions, which haunted her daily, vanished on the

first day of her fourth month of unem-
ployment.

Alicia's cell phone rang on Monday
morning. Expecting bad news, the caller
startled her.

"Hi Alicia, this is Debbie from the
Edgar Allan Poe Library on Sullivan's
Island," the caller said. "I was calling to
see if you were still interested in the administrative assistant position you applied to?"

"Definitely!" Alicia exclaimed, a
ray of hope lifting her spirits. Alicia
discussed the position with Debbie for
about fifteen minutes before scheduling
an interview for the following Monday.
During the remainder of the week, Alicia
read up on the library and its collections
and mission. Then, on the day of the
interview, she drove out early to the library to make certain she was not late.
Unfortunately, her eagerness and renewed vigor were soon dashed. One of
three finalists for the position, Alicia
was informed that the search committee
selected one of the other candidates for
the position. The interviewer informed

Alicia that they would keep her résumé on file should another job become available, but it was a small comfort as the interviewer also indicated that no other positions would be opening for at least a year. Tired, afraid and hopeless, Alicia left the library and wandered about Sullivan's Island debating what to do next. Her trek soon led her to a beachhead that faced the Atlantic. There, braced against brisk winds and the cold, salty air, Alicia looked out to the immense ocean, desperate to see beauty, purpose or peace. Yet, all she saw was isolation in the form of a bird soaring aimlessly through the sky.

"Are you as lost as me?" she whispered, not expecting an answer from the dark shape shaded in part by a growing cloud cover. As if in response, the bird shot higher into the sky before diving earthward, on a direct course for Alicia. At the last second, the bird, a seagull, diverted its flight path and landed in the surf yards away from where Alicia now stood. Alicia looked on in wonder, trying to ascertain the bird's motives. Her attention soon drifted to a bottle meandering amongst the waves, propelled by the ebb and flow of the tide. As if commanded, the bird floated to the bottle and edged it closer to shore, preventing the tide from pulling the 20-ounce bottle further out to sea. Curious, Alicia walked to the area to examine the bottle. It had no label to identify the bottle's brand, though it did have a rolled up sheet of paper stuffed inside. Stepping into the surf's edge, Alicia grabbed the bottle before retreating to higher elevations. The bird, appearing oblivious to Alicia's movements, simply continued to float about until the woman had the bottle. Then, as if satisfied, the bird flew up into the clouds and vanished.

After watching the clouds envelop the seagull, Alicia turned her attention to the bottle. Removing the cap, she quickly removed the sheet of paper trapped inside and unrolled it.

"*Anxiety, depression and misfortune are enemies we all face, enemies we cannot conquer alone,*" Alicia said, reading the message aloud. *"Be coura-geous and ask for help."*

After sitting in the sand, Alicia con-sidered the message for a longtime, questioning whether it was a good idea to admit defeat. Looking back at the ocean, she thought of the bird's appear-ance and the comfort the lone seagull brought her.

"Maybe I'm not alone," Alicia said while pondering the message. She then pulled out her cell phone and called her sister.

"Hello?" asked a familiar voice, which instantly comforted Alicia.

"Hi Lynn, how are you?" Alicia asked. She tried to sound upbeat and relaxed, but her sister knew better.

"What's wrong, Alicia? Are you ok?" Alicia remained silent, considering how to reply. "Alicia, please tell me what's wrong."

"Lynn, please help me," Alicia said, tearfully.

"Tell me where you are, and I'll be right there." In less than an hour, Lynn was at Sullivan's Island to comfort her sister. Sitting on the beach, they discussed Alicia's job search as well as Alicia's depression. Lynn immediately helped Alicia find counseling services that helped Alicia slowly bounce back from her bout with depression. Then, within a month's time, the sisters found a new job for Alicia, which provided financial security, benefits and peace of mind. On that day Lynn met her sister on the beach, Alicia said she regretted waiting so long to ask for help.

"The important thing is that you did ask for help, little sister. It's something we all need from time to time."

Chapter 12

Leland could not have been any-more different from his schoolmates, a fact they reminded him of daily. Short for his age and frail, the brown-haired, brown-eyed thirteen year old stuck of like the proverbial sore thumb. With buckteeth, braces and thick lenses to aid his sight, Leland suffered through a range of jests, which made school a re-occurring nightmare. Every single school day was the same. He went to his bus stop, where one group of kids started with the jokes, and moved on to home-room, where classmates continued to bombard him with jests, each of which cut deeply into Leland.

Occasionally he considered speak-ing up for himself or speaking to a teacher, but the fear that students would retaliate kept him quiet. To make mat-ters worse, a number of teachers in the schools he attended joined in, laughing at Leland's appearance and his difficulty speaking up in class. Leland imagined the teachers were trying to fit in with the 'popular' kids, just like everyone else. Leland reasoned he was on his own. Thankfully, home life was entirely different.

Leland's family was close-knit, spending time together whenever possible. Indeed, his best friends were his parents and his siblings, all of whom listened intently when he spoke and looked out for Leland's, the youngest, wellbeing. Petrified of asking questions during class, fearing he would look stupid, Leland found that his family was eager to make sure that he understood class material, Leland's siblings helping him with class material while his parents purchased encyclopedias and other books that further clarified course material. In many ways, Leland was home-schooled, which suited him just fine. Unfortunately, the time spent with his family seemed to fly by while the dreaded hours spent in school lingered.

With every grade, more grief piled onto Leland's shoulders. Worry of doing well on the SAT and getting into college fought with Leland's wish to ask out one of the cute girls in his class to the prom. He did do ok on the SAT, he did get into a college, but he never gathered the courage to ask a girl out for a date. He tried several times to speak to girls he developed crushes on, but Leland ultimately felt voiceless when it came to talking to girls, or anyone outside of his parents and siblings for that matter. As for talking to his parents about being bullied and teased at school, that was something Leland could not do, the only thing he could not bring himself to tell his family. He was too embarrassed to say anything, feeling it might make his parents feel they failed in some way, and Leland did not want to hurt them. So, in silence Leland went onward, attending school until graduation. Unfortunately, high school was not the last leg of his educational journey. The countdown for college began the moment he walked across the stage to receive his high school diploma as did the growing fear that he was about to endure four years of additional torment at the hands of classmates and future professors. Leland slept little that summer.

In the days before his first college course, Leland's stomach felt like its knots had knots. He worried about how classmates would treat him and wondered how he might change in order to fit in. No answers came, nor did he find sleep possible. Two days before classes were to begin, Leland tossed and turned all night until he finally decided to find a distraction from his thoughts. Grabbing his fishing gear, he jumped into his beat up Chevy Cavalier and drove out towards his favorite fishing hole, reaching it just as the sun broke over the horizon. Yet, as perfect as the morning was for fishing, with not a cloud in the sky, he never cast. Leland just sat by the riverbank, fighting the thoughts that gnawed at him all summer.

"What do I do?" he asked, pulling his knees to his chest before resting his forehead on his kneecaps. Years later, Leland reasoned that he sat in that position for hours, though he truly never remembered. What he did remember, however, was that the bird's squawking broke him from his meditation. Looking down at the water's edge, he immediately saw a floating seagull, who continually called out as if bothered by Leland's presence. "I guess that's my cue to leave," Leland whispered as he reached over to collect his fishing gear. In reply, the seagull flew up onto the riverbank and chirped repeatedly.

"I'm leaving, OK?" Leland exclaimed turning back to face the bird, but the bird was gone. Leland rushed to the river to see where the bird had flown to, but a new discovery replaced his concern for the bird; a plastic bottle containing a piece of paper rested in a patch of nearby reeds. Pulling the bottle from the water, Leland stared in wonder at the object before looking around to see who could have placed the bottle there. Seeing no one, he unscrewed the cap and shook the piece of paper into his hand. Opening the paper up revealed a message, written in the most pristine handwriting he ever saw.

"*Being who you are makes the world a better place*," he said, reading aloud the message. Flabbergasted, he scanned the area again. Had someone been listening? Placing the bottle and the message in his tackle box, Leland left the area, turning once to look back at the riverbank. All day he thought about the message, considering its implications. While still nervous about his first day of college, his hope in being accepted and appreciated by his classmates was strengthened. When the first day arrived, Leland went to his first class with most of the knots out of his stomach and refreshed from a full night of sleep. The professor began class by going over the course syllabus, focusing on the grading policy and the topics to be covered. The bottle's message played through his memory as questions about the class requirements swirled through his mind.

"I'm here for me, to learn," Leland said to himself. "My questions matter." In a room packed with college students, a lone hand, Leland's hand, raised up, drawing the professor's attention.

"Yes?" the professor asked. Leland found his voice and asked a myriad of questions about the grading policy and the term paper the class was assigned. The professor eagerly answered Leland's questions, clarifying things the professor failed to mention initially. After class, the freshman sitting next to Leland thanked him for his question; she had the same ones. In time, Leland felt at ease asking questions, recognizing that students often have the same questions, but few are willing to speak up. He also found that the minute he was comfortable with being himself, the fear of speaking and interacting with others disappeared. In little time, he had little difficulty speaking with peers and professors and found a group of friends who would ever remain like family to him.

Chapter 13

It seemed so surreal, all of it. Today, Thomas had planned to travel to Allegheny State Park for what would be his yearly fishing trip with his father. Instead, he was driving in his father's funeral procession to the cemetery.

After two days of wakes and a mass with countless somber-clothed people in attendance, it all came down to this; his father's burial. The site was pristine, picked out by his father ten years earlier for Thomas' mother, who also died unexpectedly. Their burial plot was on a hill overlooking the Delaware River, just outside of Philadelphia. The site punctuated by randomly placed silver maples, it was all picturesque, a fitting location for the two people he loved most, two people who loved the outdoors. Thomas did not remember most of the words said or sung during the Mass; he could not stop thinking of his parents being together again, a thought that brought him some solace.

"God's Will be done," he said repeatedly while gripping a set of his mother's rosaries, a now habitual act he performed daily. The movement of people around him broke his meditation; the service was over. A number of family member and friends stopped to offer Thomas words of condolence, yet he could not stop thinking of his father and their trips, which ultimately brought a smile to his face. The smile hurt. *How can I feel happy today?*

The youngest, Thomas' siblings did the heavy lifting, giving a heartfelt eulogy at Mass and arranging for a luncheon after the funeral at a nearby restaurant, where everyone gathered immediately following the service at the cemetery. Upon entering the restaurant's parking lot, Thomas could tell most of the attendees had arrived and were already inside. Part of him wished it would be just him and his siblings. He entered the restaurant from a back entrance, which just happened to open to the banquet room where his father's luncheon was. He was instantly bombarded by more condolences and hugs, mostly from people he never met.

"Thank you for attending and for remembering my father," Thomas continually replied. The praise for his father was genuine and heartfelt, which brought comfort for Thomas at such a dark time. Yet, he longed for silence and time to remember his father and grieve.

"We're almost through, Thomas," his sister told him at one point, words that helped him keep grounded. Grabbing a plate of eggs and ham from the buffet, he soon joined the head table where his siblings sat and ate in relative silence. They were exhausted, but kept standing to greet well-wishers. Thomas just sat wishing he had his siblings' strength. Occasionally he stood and greeted mourners, but Thomas found his stomach and legs were too quivery for him to keep up with the endless line of people. Then things got worse.

Thomas struggled, listening in as friends and family laughed throughout the luncheon. What began as stories of his father's accomplishments and kindheartedness soon led to people ridiculing some of his father's cars and clothes. *Why were they making fun of his father? How could they be so uncaring, so cold?* It soon got even worse. Mention of his father seemed to disappear as attendees began mingling to catch up with people they had not seen in years. People laughed about recent family gatherings or sporting events. Others, meanwhile, seemed to be making plans for joint summer vacations. Thomas could not handle it any longer. He set down the cup of tea he had been sipping and left, ignoring everyone who tried to offer condolences as he meandered through the restaurant towards the exit. In less than a minute of exiting the restaurant, Thomas was in his car and barreling down the nearby highway, no destination in mind. Aimlessly he followed road signs, detours, and finally, a lone seagull soaring high above a cemetery, the very cemetery where his parents were buried. He quickly headed to his parent's gravesite.

***

After pulling up to his parent's gravesite, Thomas exited and was immediately overwhelmed by the silence of the cemetery. Remarkably, it was not a silence tainted by death, but filled with peace. Walking over to his parent's gravesite, Thomas marveled at the fact that the hole over which his father's casket had rested was now filled. Even more amazing was the fact that his father's death date had already been engraved into the headstone.

"I miss you, Dad," Thomas said as he squatted down and ran his fingers over the inscribed dates. Then, his eyes closed, Thomas took in the growing chorus of sounds emanating from the cemetery. Sounds of chickadees chirping, squirrels rustling through leaves and the Delaware River churning brought a sense of life to the hilltop. Thomas turned and walked onto a nearby path that encircled the entire cemetery, heading towards the bank of the Delaware.

Stopping within feet of the water, Thomas closed his eyes, once again listening to the sounds of life coming from all around. A shrill cry from the seagull overhead jarred Thomas from his thoughts. Looking up, he watched the aviator dance amongst the clouds until the bird suddenly plummeted towards the water's surface. Feet before hitting the water, Thomas looking on in horror, the bird slowed its descent and landed quite peacefully on top of the Delaware River. Exasperated, Thomas bent to his knees and audibly signed.

"Thanks for the heart attack," Thomas quipped as he stared at the ground trying to catch his breath. Once calmed he looked up and stared at the bird, which seemed relatively unaffected by a river current exacerbated by a series of recent rainstorms.

"Showoff!" Thomas cried out, flustered at the bird's antics. The bird did not respond even as Thomas chuckled a bit at its theatrics. He instantly felt remorse. *How can I laugh?* Another cry from the seagull forced Thomas to look up, this time seeing a bottle near the water's edge, which the bird now floated towards. Standing by the bank, he could easily see the rolled up piece of paper inside the bottle. Thomas bent over and retrieved the bottle, shaking off the excess water before removing the cap. For long moments he considered if he should extricate the note. Curiosity got the better of him; Thomas removed and opened the paper, which read, *"Those who have passed want us to live, love and laugh."* A second after Thomas read the message, the seagull vaulted back into the sky, even as hope coursed through Thomas' heart.

"Dad!" Thomas cried out after the bird. "I love you, Dad." Thomas waited on the bank until the seagull vanished amongst the clouds. Then, his heart mended, Thomas walked back to his car and quickly drove away from the cemetery. He rejoined the party and added to the storytelling, joking with others about pranks his father played on loved ones and recalling how his father painted burned out light bulbs, adding wires for legs and arms, essentially creating light bulb people. The jokes and stories became a great release, which brought comfort. Thomas soon felt as if his parents were watching, which lightened his heart and made him smile more.

Epilogue

Time passed, and Father William Sullivan aged. Yet, the priest's mission continued. He strolled along the beach daily, searching out plastic and glass bottles to carry his messages of hope. With his compatriots, Perch and Thud, ever at his side, Father William collected an endless variety of soda, water and juice bottles, not to mention the trash that often came with the tides. Early on, he established a routine that worked well. Father William woke each morning, said a rosary or two and then shaved, using freshly split fragments of obsidian as a razor. He then washed up by the side of the pond before patrolling the beach for bottles or refuse, a task that usually took a couple hours. Father William relished the process, because the bottles and their labels provided some news of the outside world.

It was not that the labels detailed current political or economic events. The labels simply provided snapshots of the life he was missing, particularly in regards to movies, toys and junk food. As for movies, bottles often detailed contests associated with a new movie release. The advertising included information about actors and actresses involved and costume designs, or redesigns in the event the movie was a remake. Some of the movies were a big surprise.

"What more can they put John McClane through?" he asked after finding a label depicting a seventh Die Hard movie. Die Hard sequels were just the tip of the proverbial iceberg. In time, Father William would learn of two new attempts to restart the Spiderman franchise, that Rambo was not done wreaking havoc on the *bad guys*, and that Star Wars may have happened a long time ago, but it was likely to continue in sequels for a long time to come. Entertainment aside, the bottles also provided a glimpse of global economies, at least with respect to marketing strategies and consumer goods variability. For the health conscious, a variety of natural sweeteners cycled through soda companies, each touting greater taste with fewer calories. Various companies also started creating vegetable-flavored waters with a day's worth of fiber inside, flavors like cucumber, carrot, and broccoli. Additionally, packaging designs changed considerably to include a series of graduated lines, which showed the amount of calories consumed.

"They may be taking this a little far," Father William remarked the first time he encountered such a bottle. Other labels were nearly as disconcerting. Coca-Cola seemed to be trying a new "New" Coke recipe.

"You'd think they'd learned their lesson by now," Father William commented on seeing the *New Coke* label. "Stick with what works," he complained, remembering the fiasco of the first change in Coca-Cola's formula. Fortunately, the priest found some pleasant surprises, at least for his tastes. Regardless of the discoveries he made, Father William always called out the soda-news he received to Perch and Thud.

"Guys, Pepsi is making Orange Slice again!" he happily exclaimed on one occasion. Upon further examination of the 24-ounce bottle of Slice, he found additional news worthy of mentioning. "It's being bottled now in Buffalo!" Father William called out, holding the bottle high and waving it for his companions to see. In response, Thud started scratching his hind legs, while Perch groomed his left wing. Used to the cold shoulder from the bird and hare, Father William simply smiled and moved on further down the beach.

For years, Father William's beach patrols continued, and each time he found a bottle, he ripped off the bottle's label and inserted a new message of hope. Then, after morning Mass, he went to the shore and cast the bottle into the ocean, praying it would reach the person who needed it most. Time drew on, and his companions aged, as did he. Thud wandered with Father William for five years before passing. Heartbroken, Father William continued on, descendants of Thud joining the processions in the rabbit's stead. Perch, meanwhile, never strayed far from William. After ten years, William grew concerned of the bird's fate. *How would he endure after Perch died?* After twenty years, Father William cut back on his walks along the beach, an effort to spare the ancient bird. Indeed, Perch's feathers lost their luster over the years, and the bird's gait waned a bit as well. Yet, the seagull lived on. After thirty years, Father William accepted, with joy, that Perch would be with him forever; the priest and seagull renewed their daily surveys of the beach.

At fifty-five, William started to feel Time. His mission to spread hope undaunted, he continued to search for bottles and send out messages, but William suddenly needed a staff to support his walk. The priest's joints ached with every step and made sleep difficult. Yet, every morning, he said Mass before exploring the beach, Perch ever at his side.

"Spread these messages, Lord. Let them find the weary," William prayed every time he threw a bottle into the surf. Then, on a Sunday morning, on his sixtieth birthday, Father William received a surprise, which made his heart cry.

In the surf floated a bottle in which he clearly saw a message. William waded into the chilly water struggling against the tide to reach the bottle. Then, just as he was in arm's length, a wave pummeled him until William was fully submerged and dragged back towards the beach. As awareness returned, William surfaced and choked up the salt water he inhaled. There at his side, floated the bottle. Without a word, Father William staggered back to the beach where Perch waited. His initials scratched into the cap, William knew it was one of his bottles. Hope faded.

Did any of his bottles reach civilization? Did he bring Hope to anyone? Struggling to unscrew the cap, Father William wasted minutes until the message rested in the palm of his hand. Suddenly he found himself numb, unable to open the message. *What words of his*

*remained unread? What bit of hope had
he failed to spread?*

A squawk from Perch jarred William from his glum meditation. Then, unraveling the note, Hope returned.

The bottle was his, but the words on the paper were not. The message read, *"Thank you!"*

Neil O'Donnell

A life-long resident of New York's Niagara Frontier, Neil spent years developing short stories based around his life and homeland. In time, every geographical feature of the Western New York landscape morphed into the scenery of his conjured realm, which readers know as Tropal. While a student at Buffalo State College, O'Donnell started incorporating his studies in Anthropology into his writing, delving deeply into the discord and compromise that arises when societies interact. Ultimately, O'Donnell's personal and educational experiences merged to form tales where individuals and communities overcome scarcity, injustice, and war to find prosperity, equality, and peace.

O'Donnell currently resides in Lancaster, New York, balancing his time between his family, writing, and working as a college instructor and academic advisor. O'Donnell also is striving to raise awareness of Obsessive-Compulsive Disorder (OCD), a disorder he's personally battled since childhood.

www.ingramcontent.com/pod-product-compliance
Lightning Source LLC
Chambersburg PA
CBHW060124260626
47160CB00005B/2014